Mission: Stand Down

By
Shelly Mateer

Cover photo by Shelly Mateer

Published by False Buddha LLC
1314 East Las Olas Boulevard No. 232
Fort Lauderdale, Florida 33301, USA

Book layout by www.ebooklaunch.com

Library of Congress Control Number: 2017913941
ISBN-13: 978-0692948057
ISBN-10: 0692948058

This book is a work of fiction. All names, characters, places, businesses and events are either the product of the author's imagination or are used fictitiously.

All statements of fact, opinion, or analysis expressed are those of the author and do not reflect the official positions or views of the CIA or any other U.S. Government agency. Nothing in the contents should be construed as asserting or implying U.S. Government authentication of information or Agency endorsement of the author's views. This material has been reviewed by the CIA to prevent the disclosure of classified information.

Chapter 1

Jay scowled at the words from Headquarters that were displayed across his screen. He winced internally at the knowledge that his cable documenting an uncharted area in northern Konigstan was completely ignored because Headquarters had only cared that Jay had taken a "date" on a day trip. A German citizen, no less. The next cable in his queue was brief, straight from the desk officer covering his account, directing him to complete the security forms pertaining to close and continuing contact with a foreign national. He slammed his laptop shut with a loud clap and looked out at the smoggy Furstville sky, wondering for the millionth time why he left his happy, ███████████████████ to risk his life in this shithole.

A knock at the door brought him out of his self-pity. Knocks at his door never failed to elicit a bit of an adrenaline rush and visions of being taken away by the Secret Police for questioning, followed by an inevitable stay in Folter Prison.

Winston appeared in the doorway with his usual pained expression on his face.

"Uhhh… Sir. Uhhh, I have the car ready for you," he mumbled, looking down at his hands.

Jay grabbed his briefcase and bustled past Winston into the hallway, giving him a hearty slap on the back.

"And how is your family? Your son is feeling better, no?" Jay asked, pretending he cared at all about the well-being of his driver and his family.

As Winston babbled on with his usual tales of life peppered with plenty of "uhhs", Jay drifted off in thought about the tasks ahead of him. He was to ██ ██ ██ ████████████████████████████, and Jay knew that Headquarters had no idea what they were looking for. This was all just a form of busy work, because they really did not expect Jay to be successful in his work in Konigstan. They needed to keep him busy, which translated in their minds to keeping him out of trouble.

A year prior, he had been hastily directed to relocate to Furstville, ████████████████████████████████ and wait for instructions on how to proceed. He had been waiting for nine months before he began receiving requests from other divisions to scope out different areas of the country. Most of the trips seemed like wild goose chases to Jay, but he did what he was told.

He had made the best of his predicament, and enjoyed his frequent trips out of the country. He had become especially fond of visiting Germany, where he would always stop to see Sabine. He had met her at a trade show in Furstville, where she had been working a booth for her tech company. Feeling as if he had been living like a monk for months, he had spotted her immediately and after chatting for a bit, had asked her to lunch. His last female contact had been a married woman in Spain, so he found his interactions with the unmarried Sabine to be refreshing. She was a sporty type, the type of girl who liked rock climbing and hiking, and he took her on many day trips throughout Konigstan, using the travel to gather any information he could about the area and send it back to Headquarters in a series of reports. He thought Headquarters would appreciate the forward-thinking; after all, he knew they were seriously lacking information on the entire country. He was under the impression that the last ground truth type of information they had on Konigstan was from the 1970s. But instead of appreciating the work he had done, Headquarters chose to focus only on the fact that he had been accompanied by a German citizen. He was being scolded for taking a "date" on intelligence gathering trips. That would be the last time he included such details in his write-ups; from now on he would just stick to the bare minimum, not offering any extraneous information.

Winston pulled into a dirt parking lot in front of a ramshackle building that appeared to have previously been an auto mechanic's shop. He brought Jay there to introduce him to an old friend that he thought Jay might be interested in meeting. Jay wasn't sure what this was all about, but he had agreed to meet the stranger, always open to a new adventure and possible intelligence.

Jay got out of the car as a wiry, somewhat rough looking man came out to meet them, hugging Winston and exchanging the three cheek kisses that never failed to throw Jay off a bit. William then turned to Jay and the appropriate "salaams" were exchanged. William ushered them into the old building and led them to a padlocked door.

The old door swung open to reveal a long table covered with machine guns. William began explaining where he had gotten them with Winston serving as a translator. Apparently the guns had been "discovered" along the border with Kriegland. They were American weapons, and Jay wondered what had happened to the soldiers that they had belonged to.

William was offering to sell the weapons to Jay. While he was sure that this had some sort of relevance to U.S. intelligence, Jay also knew that he would open a huge can of worms if he reported this to Headquarters. Not to mention, Headquarters would have a massive freak-out. He took note of some of the serial numbers, which he knew would soon be defaced, and tried to casually explain ███████████████████████, and that he would have to pass. William did not want to let it go so easily, but Jay managed to convince him with a little bit of humor.

"I'm a lover, not a fighter," Jay explained, holding up his hands with a sheepish smile.

Winston translated this statement into whatever Konigsian equivalent there was, and that seemed to convince the disappointed William. He laughed and by studying his phone intently and frantically texting, looked as if he needed to get back to other, more pressing business.

Jay's mind was racing as Winston maneuvered the car through the crowded streets of the city. There had to be intelligence value in what he had just witnessed, but he was positive that Headquarters would not be happy if Jay got involved in weapons transactions, especially dealing with weapons that appeared to have belonged to U.S. troops. He could just picture it; he would be summoned back to Washington immediately if he wrote *that* cable.

He looked out at the gray sky and sighed. He was on his way to meet Nigel, the young kid he had been developing who had the potential to be a great new recruit. Nigel ████████████████████████████████

██

██

██

████████████████ Jay had been careful about reporting his exchanges with Nigel. He had kept his reports very basic and vanilla. He would need to tread very lightly with this one, leading slowly into the significance of Nigel's knowledge. He knew that Headquarters could be very skittish, and he did not want to scare them. Jay frowned with the knowledge that perhaps eighty percent of his time was spent figuring out how to tiptoe around subjects that Headquarters might find scary. This was not the Agency that he had dreamed of working for - the Agency of the OSS days and Cold War spy movies. It had become more like the Social Security Administration on steroids.

Chapter 2

The meeting with Nigel had gone spectacularly well. As an unexpected bonus, Jay now had an Konigstanian ████████████████ in his possession. Nigel had obtained ████████████ through his supervisor, and Jay was aware of the huge significance of this item to the Intelligence Community. He was eager to recruit Nigel - it would be his first recruit in-country - but he realized that Headquarters would require many administrative cables prior to Jay even being able to mention recruitment.

Tingling with excitement, he placed ██████████████ ████████ on a shelf in his home office. He plopped down in front of his computer, beginning to compose a cable in his head, when the vibration of his phone snapped him out of his thoughts. His irritation at being interrupted vanished when he realized that the offending vibration had been a text from Sabine. She was going to be in Kackilackistan for a trade show and wanted him to join her. He loved the luxury of Kackilackistan and was due to make a trip out of the country anyway. ██████████████████████ ██████████████████████ ██████████████████████ ██████████████████████ ████████████

He began searching flights to Kackilackistan. He would join Sabine at her hotel, where he would have his own suite. He liked Sabine, but one never knew how things could change when spending an extended period of time together. He had grown accustomed to being on his own, and even though he had always been somewhat of a lone wolf, his recent experience in Furstville had served to strengthen his loner tendencies. He would spend a few days in Kackilackistan, and then he would head off to a meeting in the States. The news of his new acquisition would be easier to convey in a face-to-face meeting with his Headquarters handler.

As he finished the short cable notifying Headquarters of his upcoming travel and requesting a meeting Stateside, he hoped it would not take them long to respond. Frequently it took Headquarters weeks, if not months, to respond to his cables, and he had scheduled his flights within the coming week. He knew they likely would not appreciate his short notice, but that is what his life as a case officer was full of - short notice and quick decisions, with little guidance.

He sat down to a meager meal of canned tuna and sparkling water while perusing the list of inane cables that had come in from Headquarters that morning. They were all of general interest, mostly vague counterintelligence, CI, guidance cables for operating in other countries. The mostly common sense guidance always made him wonder which of his colleagues had screwed up lately. Some of them were clearly triggered by a mistake made by an inexperienced officer. Mistakes were not hard to come by, as most of the officers out in the field at this point in time were very inexperienced, most just out of graduate school. There had been a push lately to get more officers out in the field, and many were not prepared for it. How could they be? For most, this was their first real job.

Jay was of a different breed. He was a little older than the others, ████████████████, and had ██████████ 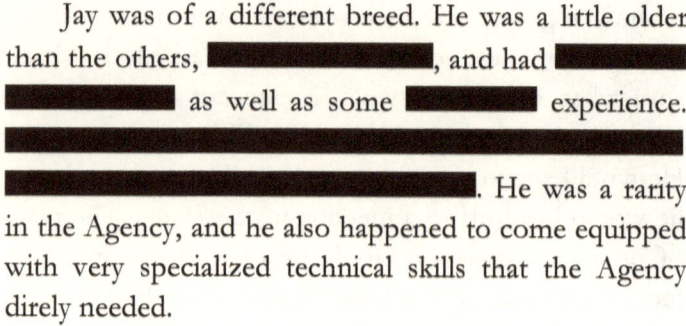 as well as some ██████████ experience. ████████████████████████████████████ ██████████████████████████████. He was a rarity in the Agency, and he also happened to come equipped with very specialized technical skills that the Agency direly needed.

And there it was, the cable requesting that he have name traces run on Sabine. Her full name would be necessary, and he did not even know her last name. He smirked at the ridiculousness of it all. He didn't intend to marry the woman!

Chapter 3

He had his laptop open to try to discourage Winston from useless chatter. It was very early morning and Jay hadn't even had coffee yet. They were on their way to the airport to catch the first flight of the morning to Kackilackistan.

Stopping at the first available kiosk to get an espresso, Jay noticed two Secret Police officers staring intently at him. They wore the customary beards and menacing scowls on their faces. Jay had shaved for his trip to the United States. He typically allowed his facial hair to grow out while in-country, but heading to the States was a different ball game. While the Americans would think he looked like a potential terrorist if he entered the country in his bearded glory, his clean-shaven face drew scrutiny from the Konigstanian security services. He kicked himself internally for not waiting to shave his beard until he arrived in Kackilackistan.

Jay took a deep breath and strode confidently past the two Secret Police officers, who followed him with their eyes. When they turned, as if to follow him, he pulled his cell phone out and placed it to his ear. He began to speak quickly in ███████ about a fictitious business deal. The officers must have heard him, because they backed off but stood watching him as he entered the security line for his gate. He had found that appearing to be extremely busy and in a hurry typically eased these types of situations. If he appeared too casual, he drew attention. If he appeared as if he did not have time for anyone or anything, people left him alone. ███████████████████████████████

Jay made his way through security with only a minor delay while a security officer inspected the bottle of rose oil that he had purchased for Sabine. When the officer realized what the liquid was, he nodded appreciatively at Jay, muttering something about the superior quality of Konigsian roses. Jay simply put on his preoccupied face and bustled through the entryway to his departure gate.

During the short flight to Kackilackistan, Jay made notes on what he would like to cover with his handler in their upcoming meeting. It was essential that he convey the importance of ████████████████ he had procured from Nigel, without inciting panic throughout Headquarters. It was a tricky situation, and he needed to tread very carefully. He would be meeting with Bill, one of his handlers, who had recently taken over contact with Jay. He liked Bill; he was a low-key guy who enjoyed visiting the Florida Keys on vacations, and talked a lot about fishing. Bill also seemed to really understand the importance of what Jay was doing, and almost seemed in awe of him.

• • •

Jay felt a blast of cold air as he stepped into the lobby of the beautiful hotel in the center of Kackilackistan's shopping district. A smile passed over Jay's face as he took in the opulence that surrounded him. He had always loved Kackilackistan, and appreciated the stark contrast between Kackilackistan and his current residence in Furstville.

His breath caught in his chest when two hands came from behind him and covered his eyes.

"Guess who?" An exuberant Sabine questioned as Jay turned, breaking free of her grasp. He felt a slight annoyance pass over him as his heart slowed back down to its regular beat. He did not like surprises; he had been constantly on edge for the past year and always needed to be looking over his shoulder.

His annoyance quickly vanished as he looked at Sabine. She was beautiful. With long, straight brown hair, almost down to her hips, and bright green eyes, she was the picture of perfection as she flashed a wide grin.

She had already settled into her suite, so Jay checked in and joined her in her room. After living without female companionship for months, he did not waste any time and began to get undressed. Sabine happily obliged, peeling her clothes off and succumbing to Jay's deep kisses.

Chapter 4

Jay lay on the bed, staring up at the ceiling, listening as Sabine appeared to be in a complex discussion with someone on her phone. He wished he understood more German. They had just returned from his favorite sushi restaurant when she had received a call that she apologetically explained that she must take. She returned from the other side of the bathroom door and casually announced that she would be leaving for China in a few days.

Jay didn't think anything of the announcement, as she traveled frequently. He grabbed his wallet off of the nightstand and shoved it in his pocket.

"Ready to go shopping?" He couldn't wait to look at all the tech gadgets. He loved shopping, and found he did not mind going with Sabine. She shopped like him; she was decisive and efficient, and she loved technical equipment almost as much as he did.

"Yes! I am ready to, how do you say, geek out," she grinned, as they bustled out into the icy cold hallway. There was definitely no lack of air conditioning in Kackilackistan.

They headed to the Kackilackistan Mall, the largest shopping mall in the world, and proceeded to spend hours gazing at all of the newest technology. Jay got a kick out of watching Sabine's eyes widen in envy at the amount of equipment he was able to purchase.

Returning to their hotel after an early dinner, Jay's thoughts were returning to the work ahead of him. He would be leaving for ████████████ in the morning, and then continuing on to the U.S. after a night in his condo. He could not stop thinking about what he needed to discuss with Bill during his meeting in the States.

Turning his back to Sabine as she snuggled closer to him under the sheets and murmured an invitation for him to spend the night in her room, he felt a familiar urge to escape. She appeared annoyed when he rolled out of bed and began putting his clothes on.

"I have an early flight," he said, as he pulled his shirt over his head.

Sabine frowned at him, but then got up, covering herself with the bed sheet as she walked him to the door.

"I will see you next time in Germany," she said as he kissed her and left the room.

In his haste to get back to his own room, he almost knocked over one of the hotel workers, who had been standing in the hallway. It crossed Jay's mind that the man had no obvious purpose for being there, but he quickly pushed the thought out of his mind and returned to the privacy of his own suite. Casting a glance over his shoulder to make sure no one had followed him to his floor, he opened the door to his suite and slipped in, relishing the quiet of the empty room. He leaned against the door for a minute, taking a deep breath of the newly cleaned hotel room air, closing his eyes as he exhaled. He couldn't explain why he always felt such a need for solitude, or why he never truly felt connected to any of the women he bedded. He had never been one for self-analysis, so he dismissed the thoughts and set his mind on work, pulling his laptop out of his bag and setting it on the desk.

He began the name trace cable that had been requested for Sabine. He resented the fact that he needed to write a cable, which would potentially be read by hundreds of strangers sitting at Headquarters, about a woman he was sleeping with. He knew that most of those strangers were practically kids, just out of college, working trainee jobs. There would also be strangers in the field, in the German stations that he was required to include due to Sabine's nationality, reading and scrutinizing his personal life.

Scowling as he sent the cable, he then slammed the laptop shut and decided to try to get some sleep. He had some long days of travel ahead of him. His brief holiday in Kackilackistan was over; it was time to get back to work.

Chapter 5

After retrieving his U.S. passport and other documents from his condo in ███████████, Jay made his way to Miami for his meeting with Bill. There was a large conference being held in the area for officers ██████████, but Jay would not be attending. Throughout his career he had managed to skip these conferences, which were held yearly and so far had not been forced by Headquarters to attend. He held a sort of special status amongst his colleagues due to the highly specialized and very dangerous work he was doing. Jay despised these conferences; he saw them as excuses for his fellow officers to get together, drink to excess, and sleep with each other. There never failed to be debaucherous tales that came out of these conferences; they were basically a big party, not to mention a huge waste of taxpayer money. Jay was not particularly against having a good time, or even wasting taxpayer money, but he had always been inclined to stay away from these conferences.

Bill met him in a beachfront hotel, situated along the main strip of bars and restaurants that catered to young spring breakers. Jay knew the timing of the conference, as well as his meeting with Bill, was no coincidence. Washington, D.C. was quite frigid at this time of year, and Headquarters officers jumped at the chance to come down to a warm climate, all on the government's dime.

Jay was a little disappointed that Bill was not accompanied by the technical expert that he had requested. Bill was a smart guy, but he did not have the expertise to understand the importance of ███████████ that Jay had recently procured.

They spent the morning going over the concerns Headquarters had about Jay's personal security in Konigstan. Bill had a lot of questions about ███████ ██████████████████████████ his residence there. Apparently Headquarters was very worried ███████ and thought that having them would draw attention to him. Jay patiently explained that everyone in Furstville had such ████████████████ their residences. The ███████████████ would draw attention. Jay tried numerous times to change the focus of the meeting by describing ████████████ he had in his possession, but the questioning always returned to the subject of the ████████████. By the time Jay was able to discuss ████████████, Bill was already thinking about where he would go to lunch. Bill took note of ████████████ that Jay described, but Jay wasn't quite sure that Bill grasped the importance of it. When pressed for suggestions on how Jay should plan to transport ████████████ out of Konigstan, Bill reluctantly offered that Jay could drive ████████████ out of Konigstan by way of the Freilandish border. However, there were a lot of unknowns with this plan, which translated into potential roadblocks with Headquarters. Just as Jay thought they were finally getting somewhere, Bill appeared to become consumed with the idea of picking up a burrito at a place nearby. Jay finally resigned himself to the fact that he would need to write a detailed cable regarding ██████████████, spelling out the importance of the acquisition and requesting input on possible ways to safely transport ████████████ out of the country. The trick would be finding the correct office at Headquarters for which to direct the cable - not an easy task as there were so many, and the acronym, or OUS, for the offices frequently changed. Jay really had no guide for this kind of thing, but he was nothing if not resourceful, and he would figure it out.

Chapter 6

Feeling a bit exasperated after his day-long meeting with Bill, Jay had walked along the beach for hours, going over the points he needed to express in his cable to Headquarters. He inhaled the salt air, taking in the scenery around him. Living in Konigstan had made him take notice of things that most people took for granted. He had a newfound appreciation for the sight of scantily clad women on the beach and males and females walking hand-in-hand. In Konigstan public affection was frowned upon, and on the beach women were required to cover their entire bodies in observance ████████████████, even while the men and children could swim and play. Visions of entirely ████████████ wading in the shore contrasted with the buxom young woman in a hot pink string bikini currently bouncing out of the waves toward him.

He spent that night in his hotel room, writing his cable to Headquarters. The next morning he would stop by to see his mother briefly before his flight back to ████████. His mother was a feisty woman, who would no doubt scold him for not letting her know he would be in town. Jay smiled a wry smile as he closed his laptop. He would touch the cable up in ████████, adding in the most pertinent offices in the address line later. Writing cables was not hard - it was figuring out which office should be the one to take action that was often the hardest part. Get it wrong, and your cable would go into a black hole.

That night Jay had a fitful sleep, plagued by terrible dreams. In one dream, Jay was shackled in a dark corner of a cell in Folter Prison, listening to the sound of a young girl screaming in a cell nearby. Once the screaming stopped, he only heard sobbing and the sound of dripping water somewhere in the distance.

• • •

Jay boarded his flight to ▓▓▓▓▓▓ with a twinge of guilt hanging over him. He had stopped by his mother's condo for a visit before heading to the airport. His mother was beginning to show her age, and was not in the best health. She was a tough woman, but she had lived a difficult life. Jay's father had been an abusive alcoholic who had abandoned them when Jay was only an infant. Jay's only male role models had been his mother's five equally drunken brothers, one of whom was particularly sadistic, and would derive pleasure from torturing animals in front of Jay. His mother had chosen to cut all ties to her family ▓▓▓▓▓▓▓▓▓ in order to give him a better life. Jay wanted to be able to be there for her when she needed him, but living so far away made that impossible. He flashed back to a simpler time, when he had spent afternoons as a child ▓▓▓▓▓▓▓▓ by watching ▓▓▓▓▓▓ television in their small living room. He remembered the sunbeam that was always present, obscuring the television screen.

It had somehow offered a sort of comfort to him, like a daily visit from an old friend. Jay closed his eyes, and for the first time in a long time, fell into a deep sleep that lasted the entire flight.

Chapter 7

Jay sat in the darkened office of his tastefully decorated condo, waiting for Rosa's response to his question. Rosa was a middle-aged woman who worked in his home office back in Northern Virginia. He had only been in the office for a brief period of time, prior to moving overseas, but Rosa had seemed to develop a soft spot for him. When he had moved to ████████, she had established contact with him via chat messenger shortly after he had settled in. Contact between them was strictly forbidden, given the differences ████████████ and the work in which Jay was involved, but Rosa had initiated the contact, and Jay did not discourage it; he felt that she might be useful at some point. A wide grin spread across his face as a list of offices that he would need to address his cable to came over the messenger. Rosa was proving to be a valuable contact.

He wanted to sign off, but first he sat through a bit of Rosa's chatter. He endured some updates of office gossip and stories about her pregnant sister, and then logged off, explaining that he needed to get some sleep. Adding some final touches to his cable, and addressing it properly according to Rosa's guidance, he sent the cable. Now, he would wait.

• • •

Returning to Konigstan was always a risky venture. Jay felt the familiar adrenaline rush as he landed in Furstville, and made his way through customs. Once through all of the lines, he spotted Winston waiting patiently amidst a throng of people. He was happy to see his loyal driver, and even listened as Winston updated him about the latest events in his children's lives.

Upon arriving back at his home, Jay began to prepare for an afternoon meeting with Nigel. It was to be a largely developmental meeting, but Jay had big hopes for the recruitment of Nigel. He felt he could recruit him that very day, but he knew he must go through the correct process, which required him to write many cables to Headquarters first. Prior to leaving for his meeting with Nigel, he checked for any response from Headquarters to his latest cable about ████████████████ that was now staring at him from a shelf in his office. There was no response yet. Jay was not surprised, but he had hoped that perhaps someone would have seen the cable and sent something back, even if it were just to acknowledge that they had received it and would get back to him shortly. But, as usual, Jay was left to function in the dark, relying only on his wits to get him through. There were no manuals or guidance to assist him in his daily life in Konigstan.

• • •

Jay sat across from Nigel at the small █████ restaurant in the heart of the city. He listened intently as Nigel described his struggle with his plans to propose to his girlfriend. Nigel was saving to buy her an engagement ring, and was having a difficult time getting the money together. Jay could not relate to this struggle, but he saw a definite recruitment opportunity here. Nigel's need for money was clearly a vulnerability that Jay could use to his advantage.

Jay was also a bit distracted by a new piece of information that Nigel had exposed. He rarely discussed his brother, who had joined the Secret Police, but today he complained about how their relationship had lately become strained. The two had been inseparable as children, and into adulthood. But ever since his brother had gotten the job with the Police, his brother had become fanatical. He had begun lecturing Nigel about adherence to strict ███████████ and did not approve of Nigel's relationship with his girlfriend, who was studying to become a doctor. Nigel seemed in need of a friend. Jay would be happy to fill that need if it meant that he would make the first recruitment inside of Konigstan ██████████.

Jay was particularly interested in a comment Nigel made about a conversation he had overheard his brother having, regarding ██████████████ the Secret Police ████████████████████████████ ██████████████████████████████████████

Nigel remarked that the brother he knew growing up would never have been part of such a thing. Jay struggled with the urge to question Nigel further about this ██████████████████████ but he did not want to appear overly interested. Nigel sadly explained that he only knew that ████████████████████████████

Riding back to his house, Jay formulated his next cable in his mind. He felt an obligation to inform Headquarters of this ████████████████. He would send them the little bit of information that he had. He could not help but feel that ████████████████████████

Chapter 8

Expecting to see only the usual download of the equivalent of junk mail in his cable queue, one short cable downloaded to his screen.

"PLEASE STAND DOWN ON PURSUIT
OF ANY INFORMATION PERTAINING
TO ███████████████████."

That was it; the cable contained no further explanation. Jay was somewhat baffled by the terse message from Headquarters. The only thing the cable accomplished, besides confusing Jay, was to confirm that there was truth to the story that Nigel had told him. Jay could not understand why Headquarters would not want to attempt to get more information that could possibly help ████████. Jay knew that pursuing the issue further could draw unwanted attention to him, but he felt it was worth the risk and that he would be able to elicit information from Nigel without ████████. The cable was clear though. He was torn between what he knew to be the right thing to do, and the desire to ████████████████ avoid being called back to Headquarters, an action that would effectively end his career.

██████████████████████████████████████

█████████ Jay decided to turn his attention to all of the administrative box-checking cables he needed to write in order to be granted permission to recruit Nigel. Hunched over his laptop, the ██████████████ seeming to breathe down his neck from its perch on the shelf beside him, Jay composed the numerous cables necessary to establish Nigel's susceptibility to recruitment.

It was evening when Jay hit the send button on the last of the string of cables he had spent all afternoon writing. He sighed heavily as he stared at the ██████████████ on the shelf. He still had no guidance from Headquarters on what he should do with the valuable ██████████. He had not even received a cable commending him on his acquisition. He smirked as he realized that, if nothing else, he was learning the art of having patience.

Having never been a patient man, he then decided to pen a plan for the transport of the ██████████████ out of Konigstan, and into the hands of U.S. intelligence. During their meeting earlier that month, Bill had offered no suggestions beyond possible exfiltration of ██████████████ by vehicle through the Freilandish border. Since Headquarters was bereft of ideas, Jay began describing the plan that he had come up with. He would create labels for ██████████, labels that resembled something that his ██████████████ ██████████████ would put on their products, and simply bring the box in his carry-on luggage during his next trip out of Konigstan. He would be sure to place a dozen or so ██████████████████████████ in the bag, along with ███████████. He had accumulated a wealth of ████████████████████ for such a purpose. Konigstanians loved ████████, and if he was asked to open his baggage, ███████████████ would spring forth, spilling out and creating a distraction. It was a very simple plan, almost absurd in its simplicity, but he knew that could be the key to averting scrutiny. If he was wrong, he would most definitely be carted off to prison, ██████████████████████████████ ████████████████████████████ Jay was satisfied with this, and excited to take the risk. He felt it was more dangerous to have █████████████ sitting on a shelf in his house. He was a foreigner living in Konigstan, and it was not out of the scope of reality that on any day the authorities could choose to knock at his door, and search the premises. It was with an odd feeling of relief that he hit the send button, and now would be left to wait for a response from Headquarters.

Waiting was one of his least favorite activities. Jay decided to busy himself with exercise. He donned his running clothes and ventured out into the polluted Furstville air. Making his way past the ██████ shops and small grocery stores, he knew he wouldn't make it far in the stifling air that burned his nostrils as he inhaled. He decided to push himself to jog to the nearest park, where he would catch his breath and head back home. The sounds of the city surrounding him faded a bit as he burst through a wall of trees out into one of his favorite parks, surrounded by high-rise buildings. One of the things that surprised him most about Furstville was its abundance of extremely well-kept parks. Upon his arrival in Furstville, he had made it a point to visit as many of these places as possible, and would compose very descriptive atmospheric cables describing the strange world in which he had found himself. He did this mostly to busy himself, in those all-too-frequent times when he was forced to wait for Headquarters to show some sign of life. He had imagined that they would be interested in as much information as he could find on this very mysterious country. But, he soon came to realize that no one was reading his cables, and he decided to stop wasting the effort.

The beauty of the park was sharply contrasted by the sight of a young teenage girl being questioned by two young men in uniform. Jay stumbled upon scenes such as these quite often, and he identified these men, who were likely only a few years older than the teenage girl, as being from the ███████ militia. Jay supposed she was not adequately ████████, or had too much makeup on, and was being harassed for it. Jay felt a pang of sympathy for the girl as he turned and began his jog back home. He thought it might be time for a trip to Germany to visit Sabine.

Chapter 9

Jay caught a glimpse of Sabine as he made his way through the airport with all of his fellow arrivals to Munich. She was on the phone, appearing to be in deep conversation. As he drew closer, a warm, wide grin spread across her face as she spotted him in the crowd, and ended her phone call. Jay felt the stress of the past few weeks in Furstville melt off of him as they embraced in the crowd of waiting people. He had hoped he would have an answer from Headquarters regarding his plan to transport the ██████████████ out of Konigstan, but so far none had come forth. The waiting was beginning to fray his nerves. His trip to Munich could not have come at a better time.

Sabine drove them along the tree-lined streets to her apartment, where they quickly undressed and fell into bed. Jay loved the simplicity of being with Sabine, and the ease at which she picked up where they had left off each time he visited her. She never asked too many questions, and did not seem to have any expectations for their future. This time he had decided that he would stay with her a couple of nights before proceeding on to his ████████████ home.

They dressed and headed down to a nearby beer garden, where they both ordered tall glasses of Bavarian beer and watched the pedestrians strolling by along with the numerous bike riders. A feeling of calm washed over him as he downed the last of his beer and ordered a second. He did not drink alcohol very often, and the beer was having the welcome effect of lightening his mood.

They stayed at the beer garden for a few hours, ordering an early dinner and feeling the temperature drop as the afternoon wore on. Jay held Sabine's hand as they walked back to her apartment, and for the first time in months, he felt completely at ease.

Back at her apartment, Jay resisted the urge to check his laptop for messages while Sabine searched for a movie for them to watch as they lounged in bed. Once she had drifted off to sleep, Jay could resist no longer. He quickly logged on to find that once again, there were no messages from Headquarters. In fact, there were no messages at all. Jay never imagined he would miss the standard CI Guidance in Zimbabwe cable, but at that moment, he did. It seemed to be taking an inordinate amount of time for Headquarters to get a response back to him. He wondered if all of his hard work was falling on deaf ears.

Unable to sleep, and not really interested in watching a movie, Jay quietly slipped into the bathroom to take a quick shower. As he placed his towel on the hamper in the corner of the room, something caught his eye. The unmistakable lump of a pair of men's boxer shorts laid crumpled up behind the hamper. As if to confirm Jay's discovery, he suddenly noticed a men's razor on the edge of the sink. Admittedly, Jay did not know much about Sabine's life; he did not even know if she had a brother. Perhaps the existence of a sibling could explain the obvious evidence of a recent male visitor to her small apartment.

Chapter 10

Jay couldn't hold it any longer. He had thought he could ignore the possibility of another man's presence in Sabine's life, but he felt himself growing increasingly agitated as the day went on. They had spent the morning in a local coffeehouse, then passed the afternoon strolling the huge farmers' market that Sabine frequently raved about. Jay found himself getting annoyed at little things Sabine did, and could not hide his displeasure. From the way she sipped her coffee to the way she fondled a melon, Jay could only feel himself shutting down, a permanent frown plastered across his face. For her part, Sabine seemed oblivious to this sudden change in Jay's demeanor.

"I'm curious; whose boxer shorts are those in your bathroom?" Jay blurted out once they were back in Sabine's apartment. He was surprised at the force with which the words came out of his mouth.

Sabine's face registered bewilderment for a split second and then she smiled.

"Oh, those must be Stefan's," she replied casually. Jay's eyebrows rose inquisitively; he was somewhat baffled by Sabine's flippant response.

"He is my boyfriend. He visits quite often from China, but I have wanted to, ah, how do you say? I have wanted to end it for some time now." Sabine scratched her chin thoughtfully and then shrugged, as if dismissing the whole idea of a boyfriend living in China. She looked back at the magazine she had been thumbing through.

Jay was dumbfounded. Thoughts raced through his mind. Sabine had recently traveled to China. Had she visited this Stefan? How long had this been going on? He had been quite the ladies man himself in years past, but he had never imagined a woman he was seeing would be carrying on a relationship with another man while he was involved with her; it just didn't happen.

As much as he tried to deny that this new information bothered him, Jay couldn't stop thinking about it. His disgust grew stronger minute by minute. He contemplated leaving that night, but his flight was not until early the next morning. When the need for food overpowered his disgust they went to dinner at a nearby restaurant. Jay found himself unable to even look at Sabine. When she innocently asked him what was wrong, the anger boiled inside of him, but he only shrugged, the frown on his face deepening.

That night he slept with his back to Sabine, waking early and taking a taxi to the airport, with no words exchanged between the two of them. He needed to get back to work. Once back at his ████████ home, he found solace in his laptop. He exhaled as he downloaded the messages from the past twenty-four hours. He would relish reading all the CI guidance cables from different corners of the world and put Sabine out of his mind.

His breath caught in his chest. He had received a very short cable granting him permission to bring the

██████████████████ out of Konigstan. The cable did not enumerate how he should accomplish this, or to whom he should plan on transferring ███████████, but he had been given the green light to bring ███████████ out of the country, and that was all that he needed.

Jay began making preparations for his trip back inside immediately. He would leave early the next day, and begin disguising ████████████████ with his own homemade labels. The thrill of finally being able to make progress on one of his projects shot through him like electricity. When his phone began buzzing with a text from Sabine, he tossed the phone onto a stack of old papers, and left the room.

He couldn't sleep that night. As he tossed and turned he thought of the many options for the transfer of ███████████ into Agency hands. He thought the ideal situation would be to pass ████████████ to an officer from Madrid Station. He had absolutely no feedback from Headquarters on what they envisioned, but this seemed like the safest way, █████████████. Realizing that sleep was not going to find him any time soon, he went into his office and put these ideas into a cable to Headquarters. He was so entrenched in his thoughts that he did not even notice the sun peeking in his windows as it rose to greet another day.

Chapter 11

The comforting sight of Winston greeted Jay as he emerged from the throng of arriving passengers. He stuffed his phone deep into his pocket as he noticed the latest text from Sabine flashing on the screen. He would eventually write her back, but for now his mind was fixed solely on the task ahead of him. Transporting ████████████ out of Konigstan was going to be a risky undertaking. If he was discovered, he would most definitely be spending the rest of his short life in a cell in Folter Prison. However terrifying that prospect was, this was the type of experience Jay lived for, and the reason he joined the CIA.

Winston was in the middle of a story about his son's back problems when Jay's phone rang. ████████████████████████████████████ ████████████████████████████████████ ████████████████████████████████████ ████████████████████████████████████

████████████ Jay answered the phone, raising one finger up in the air towards Winston, who continued talking.

████████████████████████████████████ ████████████████████████████████████ ████████████████████████████████████

██
██
██

Winston was still muttering about his son's health issues, and they were pulling in to Jay's residence.

Jay gave Winston the remainder of the day off, and after a quick meal of yogurt and a serving of tuna straight out of the can, he set to work designing the labels that he would use to disguise the ███████████████ for travel out of the country. He needed to mimic the labels ████████████████████ used on its equipment, and he planned to bring some legitimate items along with the disguised ███████████, in the hopes that this would assist ████████████ in blending in. He had some old ████████████████ that would fit the bill perfectly.

He hadn't used his creative skills to design anything tangible in a very long time, but he was proud of the final result of his work. As he printed the labels and placed them on ███████████, he felt a sense of accomplishment and a definite twinge of nervousness. He was not usually one to doubt himself, but he would not have been human if he did not wonder if the labels would be believable enough for Konigstan's airport security personnel. He pulled out a bag of ██████████████████ ██████████████ and smiled as he pictured the reaction of airport security upon the inevitable explosion of ███████████████████ from his carry-on bag. Considering the Konigstanian love of ████████████████ would provide just the right amount of diversion and add a bit of levity to a potentially dangerous situation. Beyond all else, that is what Jay hoped.

Chapter 12

Inching through the security line, Jay emptied his pockets and pushed the bag that contained the ▮▮▮▮▮ box forward onto the conveyor belt. This was the moment he had been waiting for. At that moment, everything seemed surreal, and he felt as if time was moving in slow motion. He was knocked out of his reverie when a heavyset man teetered over into him as the man balanced on one leg, attempting to pull his sock up. Jay was pushed forward into a chador-clad woman in front of him. Embarrassed, he held up his hands and bowed his head apologetically to the woman, glancing up into the eyes of the airport security officer who had been studying his bag intently as it went through the x-ray machine. Jay's heart stopped for a split second and he suddenly felt very warm. He looked over at the heavyset man who had bumped into him, who was currently in the midst of a coughing fit and completely drenched in sweat. The chador-clad woman was now blocking the progress of the line as she attempted to control her toddler son, who had gotten loose from his stroller and was trying to grab onto Jay's belt. The humor of the moment did not escape him, and he suddenly felt the insane urge to giggle.

Just as he felt he was going to lose the battle against an uncontrollable laughing fit, he spotted his bag as it popped out of the x-ray machine and joined the jumbled pile of carry-on items at the bottom of the conveyor belt. Expecting to be stopped at any moment, he gathered his bag and pocket litter and made his way past the very friendly toddler who was trying to follow him. He reached into his bag and pulled out one of the ████████████████, handing it to the child, who grabbed it eagerly, grinning up at Jay.

Making his way to the gate, Jay could not get over how easily he had gotten through security. Surely this would be the most difficult part of his journey, and he had made it through with minimal scrutiny. Of course, there was always the possibility that the Konigstanians had noticed ██████████████, and for some reason they had decided to let him proceed, knowing that they could apprehend him upon his return to Furstville. Jay pushed this thought to the back of his mind and allowed himself to relax enough to get lost in the in-flight movie.

Upon landing in Frankfurt, Jay prepared himself for another trip through airport security. He joined the mass of people in line to go through the x-ray machine, feeling confident that there would be no interest in his baggage. He noted, as usual, the seeming lack of air conditioning in the airport and the musky stench of the man in front of him as the man peeled off his blazer. At least this security line was orderly and appeared to be moving at a fast pace, Jay thought as he emptied his pockets into the plastic bin in front of him.

When his bag did not emerge from the x-ray machine, Jay noticed the very austere-looking blond security officer manning the machine summoned his colleague, an equally austere-looking female officer. After huddling together in discussion, the male officer brought Jay's bag over to where Jay stood, and asked if the bag belonged to him. Jay confirmed and was waved over to a side table, where the security officer placed his bag and donned latex gloves, his ice blue eyes boring into Jay the entire time. The man unzipped Jay's bag and a torrent of miniature soccer balls burst forth, rolling onto the table and spilling on the floor. The security officer did not appear amused. He continued to rummage around in Jay's bag, pulling out the ██████ box and the ████████ and inspecting each item very slowly.

"Herr was ist, ah, Sir what is this?" the man asked Jay, ignoring the soccer balls that continued to roll off of the table.

"Those are some ████████████████████ ███████████████████," Jay recited the words he had practiced for use with Konigstanian airport security. He tried to appear casual, yet slightly irritated by the inconvenience, ████████████ ██████████

The security officer stared at Jay with a look of contempt for what seemed like an eternity. Then he nodded and placed the ██████████████ back in the bag, and bent down to gather the stray ████████████ off of the floor. He stuffed them back into the bag and, very robotically, thrust the bag toward Jay.

Jay internally breathed a sigh of relief as he walked toward his gate. He had not expected German security to be more difficult than their Konigstanian counterparts. He was comforted by the thought that ████████████ would be out of his hands soon. He would only have one more flight and security checkpoint to get through with this potentially damaging ████████, and then it would be delivered to an ███████████ in Spain.

• • •

The remainder of the trip passed smoothly, with no extra scrutiny detected. Jay arrived in Madrid and went straight to his hotel room. He imagined he would be staying there for at least a couple of days, while the Agency arranged for someone to take ██████████ out of his hands. He envisioned this ███████████, but he would have to wait for further instructions in order to complete the transfer. For all of his reading on CI guidance, he really was not sure of how difficult the counterintelligence atmosphere in Spain could be, but he imagined he would not want to be ██████████ ████████████████████████████████████ ████████████████████████████████████ ████████████████████████████. Jay looked forward to completing the brief encounter, and getting ██████████ out of his hands.

Placing his laptop on the small table in the corner of his unusually dark hotel room, Jay prepared himself for the painfully slow download of messages that he no doubt had waiting for him. He had not checked his messages since leaving Furstville, and he eagerly anticipated the receipt of instructions from Headquarters.

Slowly, the messages filled his queue. As usual, most of them did not pertain to him, but finally, the cable he had been waiting for popped up on his screen.

"PLEASE PROCEED IMMEDIATELY TO THE U.S. FOR A MEETING IN REF A LOCATION ON REF B DATE FOR TRANSFER OF REF C."

Jay stared incredulously at the cable. Opening the reference document only baffled him further. Headquarters was ordering him to not only travel to the U.S. immediately, but to be in Miami in about eight hours, which was physically impossible. It would have been comical if it was not so asinine.

After a few minutes of rereading the cable, Jay realized that it was of no use to attempt to argue with their logic. Perhaps Headquarters knew something of which he was not aware. He then wrote his own short cable explaining that because of the time differences and travel time required, he would not be able to arrive in the States until the following day, assuming he could find any available flights. To make matters more complicated, he would need to stop ████████████ ██████████████████████, which he never had in his possession in Furstville.

After completing his travel plans for the following morning, Jay tried to get some rest, but sleep remained elusive. Sometime during the very early morning hours he drifted off into a restless slumber. He was once again met by the familiar dream of being shackled, crouched in a dank corner of a prison cell, where he could hear the screams of a young girl in the distance. The persistent dripping of water echoed loudly from somewhere in the dark. The screams ceased suddenly and Jay could hear the sound of something being scraped across the floor. Through the dim light of his cell he caught sight of a uniformed guard dragging the lifeless body of a girl into the darkness. A beam of light washed over the girl's face and her vacant eyes met his for an instant as the dripping sound became more pronounced before it morphed into the loud clanging of pots in his mother's kitchen. Jay was a young boy, sitting on the floor of their living room as his mother bustled about the kitchen, making dinner. His mother entered the living room and turned off the television before she turned toward him, revealing the face of a rotting corpse, glistening in the mid-afternoon sunlight streaming through the small window in the corner of the room. Her jaws opened and closed as if trying to communicate, but no sound emerged.

Chapter 13

Having made his way through yet another country, Jay proceeded, documents in hand, on to the U.S. He was exhausted, and by this time more than a little annoyed by his Headquarters-ordained journey through five countries carrying very sensitive, potentially incriminating ██████████████. He was looking rather scruffy at this point, not having shaved for some time, and knew he would be getting some looks from his fellow American passengers. In Konigstan it was extremely common, if not almost required, to have facial hair, but in the Western world a clean-shaven look received less unwanted attention. ████████████████████████ ███████████████████████████████████████.

In a time of heightened security concerns, he knew this trait was not particularly beneficial; he knew that at this point his stubble made him look like a terrorist.

Jay's concerns about his appearance were validated when he went through customs, where the customs agent begrudgingly allowed him entry, but only after Jay was asked an inordinate amount of questions regarding his travel.

Extremely irritated and now also very hungry, Jay made his way to the hotel where he was to meet the ████████ representative sent to retrieve ████████████.

Even with the adjusted meeting time, there was not a minute to spare. Jay despised tardiness, and he pushed himself beyond his exhaustion and hunger, to arrive at the meeting place precisely on schedule.

Jay entered the lobby of the stylish Miami hotel and scanned the entirely white interior for signs ███████ counterparts. They were usually easy to identify - the standard uniform of blue collar shirts and khaki pants practically screamed U.S. government. He was unpleasantly surprised to see a very familiar face begin to rise from one of the elegant sofas near a window. Randy Grover, a lackluster officer whom Jay had had the unfortunate experience of working with in the past, had been sent to meet with him. Grover, as he was known, had bumped heads with Jay on more than one occasion during Jay's brief time in the Headquarters area. At one point, he had even stolen a targeting idea from Jay, and passed it off as his own. Jay thought of him as a bumbling idiot, and fumed at the thought that Grover would be handling ███████ for which Jay had risked his life. Jay had hoped that Headquarters would send someone who at least had some sort of background knowledge of the type of ███████ he had procured.

"Hey, my man, nice to see you!" Grover exclaimed loudly, causing more than one of the hotel patrons to turn and look at them. He gave Jay a hearty slap on the back.

Jay forced a smile and followed Grover up to the hotel room where another officer waited to meet them. Andrew, the prototypical Headquarters branch chief, rose to greet him and offered him a drink. Jay declined, and he began to remove the box from his bag. He just wanted to complete the transfer of ███████████ and get out of there.

"Oh, you can just leave that in there," Andrew explained, "the officer from Logistics should be here shortly."

After about thirty minutes of inane small talk, where Jay came to the realization that Andrew really did not know anything about ███████████ that Jay had brought them, a short, roly-poly looking woman showed up. She also seemed to have no idea what she was doing there.

"What is this again?" she asked as she took the box from Jay and clumsily fit it into her own bag.

Jay was drained. He patiently explained what the box was, while Andrew and Grover looked out the window and exclaimed excitedly about the gorgeous pool area view.

"Oh wow, okay. I don't know anything about ███████████, but that sounds pretty cool," the logistics officer commented, before heading over to the window to join Andrew and Grover in their people watching. Grover was just commenting on how large one woman's breasts were.

Jay sat, defeated, on the sofa and stared at the television, where a daytime talk show was playing, and the man on the screen was denying the paternity of a sobbing woman's child. The logistics officer suddenly realized what time it was, and broke away from the group, explaining that she needed to get back to the office. As she was leaving, she casually announced that she would ship ▮▮▮▮▮▮▮▮▮ out in the next few days, and it would take a few weeks to get up to Headquarters. With that, she hurried toward the door, dropping the bag on the marble floor as she hustled out.

"Oh gawd, I hope I didn't just break it," she giggled, looking at Jay and shrugging.

Jay was in shock. *A few weeks? It would take a few weeks to get to Headquarters?* Why had it been necessary for Jay to travel on an immediate basis if it was then going to take weeks for ▮▮▮▮▮▮▮▮ to get to the Headquarters area? Why were Andrew and Grover there, if they were not going to then take ▮▮▮▮▮▮▮▮ with them? Surely they could either fly or drive with ▮▮▮▮▮▮▮▮ back to the Washington, D.C. area, and make it there quicker than it would take to ship it.

Grover pried himself away from the view of the pool and women in string bikinis and walked over to where Jay sat.

"Hey, can you drop me at the airport on your way out?" Grover asked with a big grin.

Jay had no choice but to acquiesce, and he found himself driving a very talkative Grover towards the airport.

"Are you hungry? Man, I'm starving. You know this area - take me to lunch somewhere. I have a few hours to pass before my flight. We can catch up," Grover babbled.

The last thing Jay wanted to do was spend more time with Grover, but he *was* hungry, so he drove to a place he knew from his past life. As he parked the rental car, images of the last time he had been at the upscale restaurant flooded his mind. It had been with his then girlfriend Clarisa, and he had broken the news that he would be leaving for a job in the Washington, D.C. area. She had not been too happy, and had consumed far too many cocktails by the end of the night when Jay drove her home. Things had gotten ugly in the car, with Clarisa apparently feeling as if she had been misled, and showing her displeasure by spitting on him. Jay had then lost his temper, pulling her from the car by her ear, and leaving her on the side of the road. He never saw her again.

They took their seats in a secluded area of the restaurant and Jay watched as Grover appeared completely baffled by the menu. Jay ordered his favorite selection of sashimi, while Grover asked the waiter if they could make him a hamburger.

"Where did you learn about all this fancy food?" Grover questioned Jay, as he bit into his hamburger and a huge glob of ketchup dribbled down his chin.

Jay suffered through the lunch, even as Grover ordered another beer once they were finished eating. He listened to Grover's accounts of life in the office, and tales of all the hot new trainee women that the Agency was bringing in. Grover was middle-aged and married, but that did not stop him from expressing his admiration of the female trainees' anatomy, and he spent quite a bit of time describing it to Jay in great detail. Jay mostly nodded and kept silent, finding only the details of changes in the office hierarchy of any interest.

When the waiter finally delivered their check, Grover explained that he did not have any cash on him, so Jay took care of the bill. If he hadn't been so tired, he would have exploded with anger at this point, but the fight had been beaten out of him and exhaustion took over. Jay then drove Grover to the airport and dropped him off for his flight.

Jay had reserved a hotel room near where his mother lived, and he planned to visit her the next day before heading back to ███████████████. Once in the tranquility of his own suite, Jay collapsed on the bed, sinking into the crisp coolness of the large billowy goose down comforter and drifted off to sleep.

Chapter 14

He woke in the early morning, feeling disoriented. The sight of his laptop sitting on the small table across from the bed brought him back to reality. He had been so exhausted that he hadn't even plugged his laptop in to charge before he fell asleep. As scenes from the previous day flooded back to him he felt a familiar surge of anger. He grabbed his laptop and channeled his increasing exasperation into a fiery cable, addressed to Headquarters. In the cable, he laid out the experiences of the past forty-eight hours. It was all there: the travel through five countries and security checkpoints carrying sensitive and highly incriminating ███████████; the apparent urgent and immediate need for him to come to the U.S.; the discovery that it would then take weeks for ████████████ that he had risked his life to deliver to be *shipped* to Headquarters; all culminating in the final humiliation of having to buy Grover lunch and chauffeur him to the airport. Reading the cable over, he decided to remove the part about his forced lunch date with Grover, but the remainder of the cable endured. Hitting the send button indignantly, he felt a brief sense of vindication as the cable was on its way. Then, almost as quickly as it had appeared, the feeling was replaced by a deep sense of remorse.

His feelings of regret only increased as the day went on. He was sure that he should not have sent that cable. He had made a huge mistake. He prided himself on his ability to control his emotions, but this time he had let them get the best of him. He wondered how Headquarters would respond, or if they would respond to him at all. Checking his messages incessantly throughout the day yielded no feedback, and he finally resigned himself to the dark mood that hung over him. Even a visit to his mother later in the day could not shake the feeling of dread that he now felt. He puzzled over how an achievement such as acquiring sought-after ███████ could be overshadowed by Headquarters maneuvers that made him question his career choice.

His mother was happy to see him, and she bustled about the kitchen preparing his favorite meal ███████. Jay noticed that she had aged since he last saw her, and he knew that under her tough exterior, she worried endlessly about him. She did not know where he spent much of his time overseas, but she seemed to sense that his living situation was not as simple as he made it out to be.

Jay tried to keep the conversation light, though he had never been one for small talk, and he found himself feeling drained by the end of the night. He bade his mother good-night, resisting her pleas for him to sleep in his old room. Driving back to his hotel, he focused on his plans for the following day. He was flying back to ███████, and he looked forward to getting back to work.

Chapter 15

Returning to Konigstan after a brief stopover at his home in ███████, Jay felt more trepidation than usual. The last time he had been at the airport was while transporting ███████████████████████, and he could not dismiss the possibility that the Konigstanian services had taken note and planned to arrest him upon his entry into the country. However, nothing happened. Jay was admitted inside with less difficulty than entering the United States.

He stared at the empty shelf the ████████ box had occupied for months and allowed himself to feel a sense of pride and accomplishment. Even if the morons he met with in Miami did not understand the significance of what he had done, there must be someone out there who would.

His next task was to complete the recruitment of Nigel. He hoped to hear something back from Headquarters in response to all of the cables he had sent in previously, culminating in the recruitment request. As far as Jay knew, it would be the first recruitment of an asset completed inside of Konigstan since ████████. It was a huge deal, and Jay wanted to be the one to accomplish that monumental task.

Jay took a deep breath as he downloaded the latest messages onto his laptop. With great interest he read the one cable of the bunch that affected him directly. Headquarters was going to be holding a meeting regarding the potential recruitment of Nigel. The meeting was called a Senior Review Panel, or SRP, and all of the Headquarters elements involved in the case would be there to weigh in and either grant or deny him permission to recruit Nigel as an asset. Headquarters was requesting that Jay write a few more cables in advance of the meeting, and even though Jay felt they were mostly redundant, he began churning out the necessary documentation.

Jay was so engrossed in cable-writing that he barely noticed when the mail was delivered. On top of the small stack of mail sat an envelope that appeared to be some sort of official correspondence. There was no return address listed on the outside of the envelope, but it had the universal look of government mail. He opened it to find a formal letter requesting his presence at an interview ████████████████████████ The letter, though clearly written by someone who did not speak English as their first language, was very straightforward, and gave him the date, time and location of where he was required to appear for the interview. Even though the letter did not explicitly state it, Jay had no doubt that the generic office name given was a moniker for an office of the Secret Police. The Secret Police was perhaps one of the most feared intelligence organizations in the world, at least by CIA standards. Jay studied the letter intently, feeling a mix of emotions. He knew that this interview would make

Headquarters very nervous, and perhaps could signal the end of Jay's career. He was in an awkward situation. The meeting was in one week. If he did not attend the interview, his absence would raise flags with the intelligence service of the country in which he was living. He would be put under a microscope, his every move watched. This would go against everything that Jay was trying to accomplish. The goal of his existence in Konigstan was to stay under the radar, not to draw attention to himself. The success of his mission depended on it.

On the other hand, if he attended the meeting as requested, he most certainly would be putting himself in an enormously dangerous situation. He would be sitting in the belly of the beast, putting on the performance of his life, a performance on which his life would depend. If the security services had any doubts about him, he most definitely would be dragged off to Folter Prison.

He struggled with the question of being candid with Headquarters, and giving them plenty of notice about the requested meeting. He felt very strongly that Headquarters would not want him to attend this meeting, and that they would agonize excessively over the fact that he was summoned for this meeting. Jay knew that this could cause some major problems for his career and his current mission.

Jay decided to use the old familiar tactic of begging forgiveness vice asking permission. He would not disclose the information about the meeting until the day of the meeting, and by the time Headquarters was aware of what had happened, Jay would already be home, the interview completed or he would be locked up in prison.

His decision made, Jay tried to focus on other tasks. He lined up another meeting with Nigel, where he would elicit more personal information and basically keep the relationship warm in anticipation of eventual recruitment. He prepared the monthly salary payments for his house staff, including Winston and the maid. Once he had completed all of the small administrative tasks that he could think of, he was left with nothing to do but wait.

Chapter 16

To fill his time with something other than obsessive worry about the upcoming meeting with Konigstan's intelligence service, Jay decided to take a day trip to Alten, an ancient capital of the Konigsian Empire. He had heard that Alten was a great tourist spot with its archeological sites, museums and universities. Nigel had once told him about Alten's power plant - one of the largest power plants in Konigstan was located in Alten. This power plant fed electricity into Konigstan's national power grid, and provided a large portion of Konigstan's electrical power. Jay was fascinated by such things and he wanted to see as much of it as he could.

Jay took a train up to Alten, and, with his very limited Konigsian, managed to find his way to some of the ancient ruins and other tourist attractions that the city offered. As he toured some of the Russian-built structures in the city, he was struck by the amount of tourists he came across. Hearing so many different languages spoken and seeing so many Dutch, German and Russian people milling around, made him feel strangely homesick. If it had not been for the ▮▮▮▮▮▮▮▮ the mostly blonde women wore draped over their hair, Jay would have thought he was anywhere ▮▮▮▮▮▮▮.

As he came around the corner of one of the old buildings, he bumped into a striking Swedish woman who was taking pictures of the structure. Looking startled, she began attempting an apology in Konigsian, but Jay stopped her by responding in English. Her face brightened as she explained she was a photographer for a popular Swedish magazine.

Jay was not one to flirt, but he knew what he liked, and he never hesitated when it came to women. He spent the rest of the day with Maja, perusing tombs and ending in the Alten Museum. Jay had not realized how much he had missed female company and he found Maja's personality comforting. She was very quiet, but had expressive eyes that seemed to peer into his soul. As fragile as she appeared, she clearly was very brave to be traveling around Konigstan by herself.

They found the huge power plant and Jay stood transfixed as he stared at the high metal gates surrounding the plant. The security guards did not seem amused and waved them on when they began taking pictures of the site. In addition to architecture, Jay was fascinated by infrastructure and what it took to run a city.

As the day drew to a close, Jay was saddened at having to say goodbye to Maja. They exchanged contact information and Maja explained that she would be heading to Furstville next, for a very brief visit. Jay hoped to see her in the future and already had visions of visiting her in ██████ during one of his trips out.

• • •

Sitting in front of his computer, staring at the blank screen, Jay could not shake the image of Maja, strolling the ancient streets, sunlight gleaming on the strands of blond hair that inevitably fell ████████████ as she walked. He had never quite felt so drawn to a woman before. He suddenly began to feel very foolish and he forced himself to begin typing an atmospheric cable to Headquarters about his day trip to Alten, omitting any reference to his chance encounter with a beautiful Swedish woman.

Chapter 17

Jay awoke to a text of a picture Maja had taken without his knowledge. It was a picture of him standing in front of the power plant's large gates, staring up at the structure in awe. Jay smiled, and felt upbeat for the first time in weeks. She was arriving later that day, and Jay planned to pick her up at the train station. He had heard little from her, besides receiving a few pictures of various sites she had visited on her own since they had parted in Alten. She seemed to be a woman of few words, who expressed herself through photography. Jay found this quality enchanting and he spent much of the morning planning their day together. It was not often that he had the opportunity to play host, and he relished the idea of showing Maja around and inviting her into his secluded world.

Jay spotted her immediately, exiting the busy train station, one small bag in hand. She was hard to miss; she practically glowed, and it did not go unnoticed by the people milling about outside of the train station. She did not appear to notice as people stopped to stare as she walked by. It was not that she was particularly tall, or wore inappropriate clothing for the location, or stood out in a way that one would typically think of - it was more that she was so pale that she appeared translucent, ethereal. Even with her golden hair

████████████████, it was clear she did not belong there.

Winston seemed to forget where he was for a minute as she got into the car with Jay.

"Maja, this is my driver, Winston," Jay introduced them as the color rushed to Winston's face. He nodded and mumbled a greeting as a shy smile spread across his face.

Maja appeared not to notice, smiling warmly at Winston. "Very nice to meet you Winston. Thank you for picking me up today. It is so nice to see you again, Jay," she said turning her attention to Jay's attentive gaze.

"Are you hungry? I know a great place," Jay began, realizing he was staring at her a little too intensely. He wasn't sure what had come over him. Perhaps his solitary lifestyle was beginning to get to him. He was no stranger to beautiful women - he had been with some of the most beautiful women in the world - but this one just seemed to throw him off and he needed to regain some sort of control.

"I ate before I left, but thank you. Would you like to start at Majestic Tower, so I can get some views of the surrounding city?" Maja requested, her eyes brightening at the thought of the photographs she could capture.

Jay would have agreed to anything she said and he instructed Winston to proceed to the tower. They maneuvered their way through the congested Furstville traffic, Jay pointing out certain notable sights along the way. Maja would only be there until the next morning,

when her flight would take her back to Sweden and Jay
wanted to show her as much of the city as he could.

The day flew by in a bustle of museums, palaces,
towers and finally, parks. Jay felt as if they had done
everything they could possibly do in Furstville besides
skiing in the mountains north of the city. They ended
the day at one of the more upscale restaurants in the
city and arrived back at Jay's place exhausted.

Jay had prepared the guest room for her stay. He
did not want to appear as if he expected her to sleep
with him. He, of course, wanted very much to sleep
with her, but something about her restrained his usual
boldness. After admiring the night skyline of the city in
comfortable silence for quite some time, she simply
turned to him and kissed him goodnight.

She left for her flight early the next morning.

Chapter 18

Jay stood in front of the unmarked door and took a deep breath. As often happened in stressful moments, a strange and inappropriately timed memory suddenly popped into his head. Standing in formation at a beginning yoga class that one of his past girlfriends had taken him to, he was admiring the very attractive yoga instructor. The instructor moved around the room assisting the students with each new pose as it was introduced. As the instructor lightly pushed on Jay's back to guide him into the correct posture, Jay had taken a deep breath and, as she pushed his spine into place, Jay had suddenly broken wind, very loudly. The entire room had gone silent before everyone had burst into gales of laughter. Jay and the yoga instructor had ended up dating for a year after that.

Jay walked into the room and approached the glass-enclosed reception desk. There was no one sitting behind the frosted glass and Jay stood there for a few minutes to see if anyone would appear before taking a seat in one of the folding chairs behind him. Except for the camera positioned in the far corner of the ceiling, Jay was alone in the room. After twenty minutes of studying the scuffed tile floor, a man appeared in the doorway and motioned for Jay to follow him. Ushering him into a dark, dusty office that smelled of something

Jay could not identify, the man took his seat behind a large desk, and began flipping through a stack of papers in front of him.

"Please, take a seat," the man said, without looking up from the papers.

Jay did what he was told and waited while the man appeared to be reading something of interest buried in the stack of papers. Jay looked around the room, wondering if these would be his last few minutes of freedom before he was escorted to prison.

"Mr. ████████. Thank you for coming today. I will need you to fill out these papers before we begin the interview," the man said, handing Jay a thick stack of forms.

Jay took the paperwork and the man motioned for Jay to pull his chair closer to the desk while he cleared a spot for him to complete the paperwork. The forms began with an extensive biographical section where Jay was to enter his own information. The rest of the typical government forms asked for ████████████ ██ ████████████

Jay sat hunched over the forms for what seemed like hours while the nameless government official sat across from him, hunting and pecking his way through some report on his computer. The silence in the room was only punctuated by the man's loud breathing and occasional grunts as he examined what he had been typing.

Jay did not have all of the information that was requested in the forms, but he knew that ████████████

██████████████████████████████

██████ He gave what information he could, ██████

██████████████████████████████

██████████████████████████████

██████████████████████████████

██████████████████████████████

██████████████████████████ The idea that he ████████████ would come under a microscope made him nervous, but he did not see any way around the process.

When he had completed the forms, he handed them to the man across from him, who began questioning him about each ████████████ listed in the paperwork. He questioned him about what type of business he had in Konigstan, how that business had come about, his personal life and use of alcohol, and how he viewed the country of Konigstan and the King in general. By the end of the interview, Jay had been there for hours. The man questioning him did not appear to have any reactions to anything that Jay told him. He was completely unreadable.

At the end of the questioning, the man left the room for an agonizing amount of time. Jay tried to appear as calm as possible, aware that he was being filmed by the camera he spotted in a corner of the room. Inside Jay was anything but calm and images of being dragged off to prison filled his head. He had sent a brief cable to Headquarters about his requirement to attend the meeting just before he had left his house. He felt a bit of comfort in the fact that at least the Agency would be aware of his final whereabouts, should he disappear.

The man finally reappeared in the doorway, where he stared blankly at Jay for a minute before walking behind his desk and flipping through more paperwork. He then looked up at Jay and told him he was free to leave.

"We will be in touch," the man said, taking his seat once again.

• • •

Jay went home and immediately wrote up the details of the interview, attempting to downplay the significance of the meeting as much as possible. ███████████████ ███ ███ ███ ████████████████████

On the other hand, if ██████████████████, he was not sure how that would play out. Jay expected that he would continue operating as he currently did, ██████████████████████████████████████ hoping to remain under the radar of the Konigstanian intelligence services. This, of course, would become increasingly difficult now that he ███████████████ was being scrutinized by the Konigstanian government.

Prior to going to bed, Jay downloaded the latest cables from Headquarters. He had received a very brief cable in response to his news of the meeting he had attended that day. The cable did not say much, just that Headquarters appreciated being notified of the meeting.

Jay knew that there had to be more that had been left unsaid. At this point, he was pretty confident that Headquarters would have warned him against attending the meeting, had they known about it beforehand. He imagined that the CI people at Headquarters were probably scrambling to figure out what to tell him.

Chapter 19

His phone was ringing. Jay answered it to find ████████████████ on the other end. ████████████
██
██
Jay ███████████████████████ began preparations for his next trip to ██████████. He would have time for a visit to his condo ████████████████████ in Konigstan. He hoped he might even be able to see Maja in ██████████.

He had not heard from Maja since she left. The last contact had been a photo of the Furstville skyline that she had sent from the airport as she was waiting to board her flight back to Sweden. Jay had been so preoccupied with the Konigstanian security service interview and the lack of response from Headquarters that he had not been concerned with Maja's whereabouts. In the brief amount of time he had known her, he could tell she was not much of a verbal communicator, and he appreciated that. He hated nothing more than a clingy woman.

Jay sent Maja a text with his travel plans and invited her to spend some time with him while he was in ██████████. He offered that he could come to her, or she could come visit him at his home. Should she be able to make the trip, he would pay her expenses.

Headquarters had finally approved Jay's request to recruit Nigel and Jay planned to hold the recruitment meeting upon his return to Furstville. He was finally beginning to see some progress and his career was on track. Confidence soaring, he left for his trip to ▓▓▓▓▓▓▓▓.

Chapter 20

Taking a breath of his freshly cleaned condo, Jay placed his bag on the floor. His maid had just been there and she had stocked his refrigerator with groceries to get him through a few days. Jay was famished, and he made himself a sandwich before retreating to his office to check his email. His phone had been turned off for the flight and he expected to see a text from Maja upon switching it back on. He was disappointed to find no communication from her. He decided to give her until later that evening and then he would call her. He knew she did not like talking on the phone, but he was beginning to get worried. He spent the remainder of the day getting his paperwork in order ████████████ ████████████ in Konigstan.

By evening, Jay called Maja's phone, but after many rings, it went straight to voicemail. He wondered if perhaps he had fallen prey to another married woman. Deeply annoyed by this thought, he decided to distract himself with a movie. He turned on one of the latest in a series of movies about an apocalyptic zombie virus infecting the earth, and soon was fast asleep.

In his dreams, he was visited by the young female prisoner he had last seen dragged off by one of the prison guards. She was trying to tell him something, and her glassy eyes pleaded with him from behind rusted prison cell doors. Her mouth moved, but Jay could not hear any sound aside from the loud dripping of water somewhere nearby. He tried to stand up and move closer to where the young girl sat, but as he tried to get up, he realized he was chained to the floor, his tattered clothing soaked with a substance he could not identify. He raised one arm up to a sliver of light coming in through a barred window high above him and saw that he was covered in blood.

• • •

Reading the latest download of cables from Headquarters, none of which pertained to him, something on the muted television screen caught his eye. He grabbed the remote and quickly turned up the volume on the flat screen that hung on his wall. An image of a woman with blond hair posing on the edge of a rocky cliff somewhere, ocean waves churning far below her, flashed on the screen. The picture appeared to be a few years old, but Jay recognized her immediately.

Maja!

The news story was brief, but it described the disappearance of his photographer friend while trekking through Konigstan and implied that she may have been detained by Konigstanian security forces. Jay flipped through the other international news channels, but did not see any further coverage of her disappearance.

Jay slumped back in his chair, staring blankly at the wall. He would have stayed like this for quite some time had he not heard a noise coming from his computer screen. It was Rosa, from ████████████ Northern

Virginia. She was asking if he was okay, and Jay decided to answer her, despite feeling an incredible need to shut his laptop on her flashing query.

"I was worried about you. They are switching you to a different ██████████ - have they told you?" Her message came across the screen in the annoying hot pink that she used for her messenger correspondence.

Jay had not known about the ███████ change, but he was not concerned with any ███████ administrative changes that Headquarters made ██████████. He only hoped that they communicated any changes he would need for the correct direction of his cables.

"Rahim has been on the warpath lately. He is trying to make it seem like you have gone rogue or something," her chat continued.

Rahim was a former co-worker and rival of Jay's who had always displayed large amounts of professional jealousy toward him. Rahim had wanted the assignment that Jay had ended up getting and he had clearly not gotten over it. Now, from what Rosa was describing, he was attempting to undermine Jay's activities in an effort to make him appear reckless and unstable. Jay knew that this could be career poison. He was not there to defend himself and jealousy had always permeated the CIA workplace.

After his unsettling conversation with Rosa, Jay decided to get out of the house.

Chapter 21

Listening to the waves crashing around him, he watched as a small crab inched its way up the side of the rock where he was perched. He had always loved the ocean, with its offer of solace in times of distress. More than the news about Rahim's backstabbing, Jay was consumed with the question of Maja's fate. He had barely known her, but he felt deeply connected to her. Now, the image of her shackled in a damp, dark cell haunted him.

He sat on the rocky edge of the beach for hours, watching the windsurfers blow by on the blustery waves. He admired and envied their freedom. There had been a time in his life when he had been one of them and he yearned to get back to that lifestyle. He wished he could have remained ignorant to all of the horrible realities of the world in which he found himself currently entrenched.

He returned to his condo in the evening, sticky from the salty air. Prior to finally falling asleep that night, he made the decision to put Maja out of his mind and to focus intently on his work. There would be ██████████████████ in Konigstan in a few weeks, ██.

There was no way he could help Maja, and dwelling on her disappearance would only distract him from his purpose.

• • •

Staring numbly at the screen, Jay struggled to comprehend what he was reading.

> "PLEASE STAND DOWN ON ANY AND
> ALL TRAVEL TO KONIGSTAN. DO
> NOT, REPEAT DO NOT ATTEMPT RE-
> ENTRY NOW OR AT ANY TIME IN THE
> FUTURE. REGARDS."

Jay had grown accustomed to the brevity and curtness of Headquarters cables, but this one shocked him. How was he to never enter Konigstan again when he had a home there and a staff that depended on him for their living? Not to mention he was just breaking ground ▋▋▋▋▋▋▋▋▋▋▋▋▋▋▋▋▋▋▋▋ ▋▋▋▋▋▋▋▋▋▋▋▋▋▋▋▋▋▋▋▋▋▋▋ ▋▋▋▋▋▋▋▋▋▋▋▋▋▋▋▋▋▋▋▋▋ ▋▋▋▋▋▋▋▋▋▋▋▋▋▋▋

As if on cue, Jay's phone began ringing. ▋▋▋▋▋▋▋▋, and Jay would have to think fast.

"Hello," Jay began ▋▋▋▋▋▋▋▋▋▋▋ ▋▋▋▋▋▋▋▋▋▋▋▋▋▋▋▋▋▋▋▋ ▋▋▋▋▋▋▋▋▋▋▋▋▋▋▋▋▋ ▋▋▋▋▋▋▋▋▋▋▋▋▋▋▋ Jay listened, ▋▋▋▋▋▋▋▋▋▋▋▋▋▋▋▋▋▋ ▋▋▋▋▋▋▋▋▋▋▋▋▋▋▋▋▋▋ surely Headquarters would reconsider their decision once they realized that Jay would need at least one more trip into Konigstan in order to properly close out ▋▋▋▋▋▋▋▋▋

"I am in ███████ now. I will plan to be back in the country ███████████████████████ on those dates. I have a family emergency at the moment that needs my attention, but I expect things will clear up by then," Jay offered, ███████████████████████ ██████████████

███████████████ sounded rushed and did not acknowledge Jay's mention of a family emergency. Jay knew he would need to convince Headquarters of the importance of his being in Konigstan in time ███████████████

He sat down and began a response to the latest cable from Headquarters. In it, he tried to express the necessity of entering Konigstan at least one more time. He explained that there would be ███████████████ ███████████████████████; he also needed to pay his staff, sell his car and give notice to his landlord. There were many other things that would need to be done - he had a life in Furstville. He could not just disappear, if for no other reason than ███████████ that he had worked so hard to create, ███████████

███████████████████████████████
███████████████████████████████
███████████████████████████████

███████ He would never be able to work the Konigstani-an target, one of the most important intelligence targets, ever again. His credibility would be demolished. He would have to start over. He might even be banished to a Headquarters job.

He carefully crafted his cable to avoid sounding whiny at any point, but he was feeling increasingly frantic with each word he typed. He ended the cable, hoping that someone at Headquarters would realize the importance of his presence in Konigstan. He wondered if Headquarters could possibly know something that they were not saying. ███████████████████████

███████████████████████████████████

███████████████████████████████████

There was nothing left to do but wait. An absurd thought crossed Jay's mind as he stared out of his window at the surrounding city, the city that he loved.

At least I never adopted a dog in Furstville.

During his early days in Konigstan, Jay had toyed with the idea of adopting a dog. Konigstan was not a particularly dog-friendly environment and stray dogs were often shot on sight or killed in very inhumane ways. One morning, Winston had spent an entire car ride complaining about how his daughter wanted a pet dog, but religious leaders claimed that dog ownership was ██████, or forbidden ████████████. Winston, a doting father, had explained to his tearful daughter that dog walking had been prohibited, and it would not be fair to keep a dog cooped up in their small apartment. He had told Jay about a rare dog shelter just outside of Furstville and on one exceptionally long day of waiting for Headquarters to acknowledge Jay's existence, Jay had asked Winston to take him to the shelter.

Pulling up outside of the desolate building that housed the shelter, Jay had recalled a dark memory from his childhood. One afternoon, woken from a drunken slumber, Uncle ███████████ had become enraged by the persistent barking of a neighborhood stray. Jay watched in horror as his uncle produced a switchblade, and trapping the dog under his legs, had begun slicing the dog's flesh as it screamed in pain and tried to wriggle free of ███████████ grasp. At five years old, Jay watched in shock as ██████████ left the dog, still alive but cut in pieces, to die a slow death in the dirt outside of their house. The dog had been one of Jay's favorites, and he had often smuggled table scraps out to the dog.

Haunted by this vision from his past, Jay had asked a confused Winston to take him back home. He questioned whether he could ever have a pet if it meant that he would have to watch the animal suffer at any point in its life.

Chapter 22

Two weeks passed with no response from Headquarters. Jay had successfully avoided ██████████████, but he knew he could not use the excuse of a family emergency much longer. He had sent a cable requesting guidance on how he should handle his ████████████ ████████████████████████████████████ in Konigstan. Jay had previously described the importance ██████████████████ in the most clear and simple language possible. He knew that there were few at Headquarters who could understand the complex, technical details that he dealt with on a daily basis. ██ ████████████████████████████████. He received no response.

Jay toyed with the idea of heading into Konigstan without Headquarters' knowledge. He discarded this idea, telling himself that Headquarters must know something that they were not telling him. He liked to think that his employer was not as completely clueless as they often appeared. If he did go in without their knowledge, he would be lucky if all he lost was his job and not his life.

As the day ██████████████████████ drew nearer, Jay grew more and more frustrated. He passed his time looking into refresher windsurfing classes at the local beach and became obsessed with buying a huge recreational vehicle in which he could live. It was a somewhat preposterous idea, especially in ████████ where the price of gasoline was astronomical. But the lure of dropping out of society and out of the CIA's grasp forever was enticing. It was a fantasy that his mind kept returning to more and more often.

One afternoon as he was perusing ads for giant RVs, he received a cable from Headquarters. The cable did not relay any new information; it only reiterated that Jay should not, for any reason, go back into Konigstan. It offered no guidance or instructions on what he should do about the increasing calls he was receiving from inside Konigstan, or how he should explain his absence ████████████████████████

Jay spent the day ██████████████████ shades drawn, staring at his cell phone despondently. The phone rang incessantly. ██████████████

████████████████████████████
████████████████████████████
████████████████████████████
████████████████████████████
████████████████████████████
██████████████████
████████████████████████
████████████████████████████
████████████████████████████
████████████████████████████
████████

███████████████████████████████████

██

██

██

██

██

██

██

██

██████████████████

████████████████████████████████████

███████████████████████████████████████

███████████████████████

"Where the hell are you? █████████████████

██

█████████████████████████████████

"I know, I know, █████████████████████████.
I'm sorry," Jay began, ████████████████████

"What do you mean 'I'm sorry'? █████████████

██

██

██████████████████████████████████

████████████████████████ Jay knew he was
sounding very foolish, but he could not think of any
other excuse at this point. ██████████████████

██

████████████████████████████████

██

██████████████████████

Chapter 23

Jay gazed forlornly at his laptop, ████████████████
████████████████████████████████████
████████████████████████████ the laptop which
he used for his covert communication with Headquarters
and which contained Top Secret documents. ████████
████████████████████████████████████
████████████████████████████████████
████ Jay knew he was screwed.

Headquarters had gone silent. Jay had hoped he
could trigger some concern with daily updates on his
meetings ████████████████ and the likely consequences
████████████████████████ Headquarters
appeared to remain unmoved by his predicament.

Feeling completely hopeless, Jay was grabbing his
water bottle and beach towel to head out to his
windsurfing class, when a cable showed up in his queue.
Headquarters had awakened from its slumber and was
requesting a meeting with Jay in the States. He was to
report to the Washington, D.C. area in a few days.

Jay knew this news could not be good, but he was
glad to at least hear something from Headquarters.
Perhaps they would have some guidance for him, or a
plan to extricate himself from Konigstan without
arousing suspicion. He began packing immediately.

Chapter 24

The man sitting across from him leaned forward, his hands on his knees. Steve Resnick was the deputy division chief for Konigstan Operations Division. Jay had half expected them to bring out the Director of the CIA to sit down with him, the way they had been telling him how important the work he had done was to the Intelligence Community. He noticed they were using the past tense in their descriptions of his work and Jay knew that this did not bode well for his continuing presence in Konigstan.

Jay was growing tired of the rhetoric and had asked the question that had been burning inside of him for weeks: Did the CIA have some concrete reason to think that the Secret Police knew who he was, placing him in imminent danger?

"During a routine scrub of all of our officers' cover, we discovered that the necessary due diligence was not completed on, not only your cover, but quite a few officers in the field. In your case, we uncovered a pretty substantial ▮▮▮▮▮▮▮▮, and we just cannot take the risk of the Secret Police discovering your true identity," Steve exhaled the words as if they were a burden and leaned back in his chair again.

"███████████? What did you find?" Jay asked incredulously.

Steve pulled a pair of thick-rimmed glasses from his side pocket and put them on as he gestured to the portly woman beside him to hand him the papers she held in her lap.

"It appears that there is ████████████████████ ████████████████████████████████" Steve looked at him with a blank expression. He seemed as if he would rather be anywhere but sitting across from Jay at that moment.

"A ███████████████ that you knew about when you hired me," Jay began, trying to remain respectful while realizing all of his current troubles were due to an Agency mistake.

"Perhaps we were a bit hasty in sending you to live in such a dangerous environment. The pressure was on to increase coverage in the area, and some steps were not taken, or they were missed along the way," Steve continued. "We just cannot take the risk that the Secret Police will not discover this ██████████. Should you be imprisoned, ███████████████████████████████ ████████████████████

Jay knew the risks, and he was willing to take them. He did not think it likely that the Secret Police would dig through thousands ████████████████████ in order to research his background. No intelligence service on earth had those kinds of resources. The ████████████ was a different story, but Jay had assumed that the Agency had some way to work around that part of his past.

"I have a household in Furstville - staff, a car, numerous things that I need to take care of there before I can leave. I can't just vanish without looking really suspicious. If my cover is not already blown, it certainly will be if I leave the way you are suggesting," Jay explained, thinking of the people who relied on him for a living and some of his treasured possessions that remained in his deserted house.

Steve just stared back at him for a long while before announcing that he had a luncheon to get to. It was clear to Jay that he had not thought about the life that Jay would be leaving behind in Furstville. Nor did he appear concerned about the effect all of this would have on Jay's cover and his future with the Agency.

Upon Steve's exit, Jay was turned over to Valerie, the portly woman who seemed very anxious in the deputy chief's presence. She handed him a piece of paper and smiled warmly at him.

The paper contained the traces on Sabine. He had been granted permission to date her. Jay resisted the urge to laugh.

Chapter 25

Jay felt drained as he returned to his hotel room in Northern Virginia. Valerie had proven useless in providing guidance on how best to extract himself from Konigstan. In fact, it seemed as if no one had even considered his life there or the damage his absence would cause to his cover. He was supposed to return for another day of meetings, and he did not have much hope that those meetings would be any more substantial than the hours he had wasted earlier. Jay was beginning to think that his career was over before it had really even begun.

He shut his phone off and avoided his laptop by making a stop at his favorite sushi place in the area. His phone had begun ringing almost constantly, with calls from inside Konigstan increasing dramatically. He could always identify the Konigstanian callers, because the numbers came through as unknown. The sick feeling in the pit of his stomach was getting worse with each unanswered phone call.

Returning to the hotel lobby, Jay decided to further delay the return to his room by having a couple of beers at the hotel bar. He would engage in one of his favorite pastimes, people watching.

"Well, hello stranger," a familiar voice broke through Jay's thoughts. He turned to see the smiling face of Allison, as she pulled up a seat next to him, tossing her car keys and cell phone on the bar.

"Allison? Hey, how are you?" Jay pulled her into a hug and was surprised at how happy he was to see her. Allison had been one of the bright spots in his training experience at the Farm. Or, perhaps it was more accurate to say that *he* had been a bright spot in Allison's training experience. Jay had loved his training days. He had moved himself into his quarters at the Farm as if he was moving into his dream home. He was the life of the party those days, setting up a bar in his room and frequently holding large gatherings of his fellow trainees over the weekends, whenever their grueling training schedule would allow. Allison had been rather timid at the beginning and somewhat insecure about her operational abilities. She wasn't the most attractive girl, but Jay had found something about her alluring. They had quickly become bed buddies, more as a way of releasing tension than from any sort of romantic feelings or attraction. Most, if not all of the trainees at the Farm had such arrangements, even the married officers. Some of the female trainees would even sleep with their instructors. These instructors were mostly much older washed-up case officers attempting to relive their philandering days at stations overseas and enjoying the supposed adulation of the young women who would do anything to receive a passing grade in the class.

Jay and Allison had fun, and Jay liked to think that he had brought Allison out of her shell. Now, looking at the new lines on her face and the dark circles under her eyes, Jay wondered if the life of a case officer was truly for her. He was seriously questioning his own career choice at this point in time.

Allison ordered two shots of tequila, finished them both off with flourish, and turned to Jay.

"I'm sleeping with my COS," she blurted out, as she ordered another shot.

"How did that happen? ███████████████..." Jay trailed off. ████████████████████████ ██ ████████████████████████ He suddenly realized she had become a dreaded ██████████████. It was a fate that ██████████████ officers tried to avoid at all costs. Many times the new young officers were not cut out for the ████████████████████████ entailed.

"Yep, I'm ████████████████████████ I was a failure as a ████████," Allison slammed back another shot, and this time Jay ordered them each a shot of whiskey.

"Well, I suppose it could be worse," Jay tried to console her, but he knew he would never want to ██████████. He knew that for ██████████, the path always led back to Headquarters, and he could not even imagine having to work there.

"He's married too. And not even cute. Anyway, his wife found out and now I am back here for "consultations". He gets away with it, while I am probably destined for a desk job back here."

Jay noticed Allison's speech was slurring and she was having a hard time sitting on her barstool without slipping off of it. He wasn't sure why he did it, but he invited her to come up to his room to continue the conversation. He was starting to feel the effects of the alcohol, and he supposed he could use some company that night.

Allison appeared more than happy to accompany him up to his room and they stumbled off to the elevator. Jay noticed that she had put on a few pounds since he had last seen her. Life in the field had not been kind to her.

As they entered Jay's hotel room, Allison turned to him and pushed him down onto the bed, hiking up her skirt as she straddled him. Jay was used to being the aggressor in sexual situations, but he was suddenly feeling very tired and allowed her booze-soaked breath to envelop him as she unzipped his pants.

Suddenly, she pulled back and lurched forward somewhat violently all at the same time, and Jay was covered in a very warm liquid. She collapsed on his chest in a heap of brown hair and vomit. The stench was more than he could take and he felt himself gagging as he pushed her off of him on the bed, where her vomit began to blend in with the floral pattern on the comforter.

Chapter 26

Elegant buildings overlooking the deep blue ocean of his ███████████ home offered a sort of calm as his flight began its descent. The last day of meetings had been no more fruitful than the first, and Jay had left feeling more than a little discouraged about his situation. He had mentioned the likelihood that his ███████████████████████████████████████, but had only been met with the now familiar blank stares of his colleagues at the CIA. He had tried his best to impart a sense of urgency in this matter, ███████████ ██ ██ ██████████████. Valerie and her very young companion at the meeting had only offered that a meeting ████████████████████ would be convened in the future. Jay only needed to wait.

Sitting at the kitchen table in his condo, he stared at an old bottle of absinthe that someone had given him years ago. He was not even sure who had given him the gift, and a sad smile crept across his face as he thought about how many lives he had lived beyond his ██████████ years.

A single envelope sitting on the kitchen counter suddenly caught his eye. His maid must have brought the mail in for him while he was gone. Picking up the unmarked letter and opening it slowly, a single piece of typewritten paper greeted him with some unexpected news. ████████████████████████████████

Chapter 27

"Are you going back out?" The girl tossed her goggles on the ground next to him and looked at him with huge brown eyes. Jay nodded and held up a finger to indicate he would be joining her on the waves in a moment. With a wide grin, she turned and jogged back to the breaking waves, spraying him with droplets of salty water as she departed. He watched her tan legs as they trotted toward the ocean.

It had been a month since his last communication from Headquarters. The news of ██████████████████ ███████████ had been met with silence. He had spent the month dodging almost constant phone calls ████████ ████████████████████████████████. It had been a month of reading and rereading the latest CI Guidance for Ouagadougou cable and feeling extreme guilt about his inability to pay Winston's salary to ease his growing financial crisis.

His phone began buzzing with an unknown caller. Jay looked at the screen for a moment before gently holding the power button down until the screen went dark. Tossing the phone onto his sand-covered beach towel, he ran toward the crashing waves and dove into their cool darkness.

About the Author

Shelly Mateer is a former CIA officer. She attended the University of California, Davis where she earned a degree in international relations. Shelly grew up in various U.S. locations and overseas. Her first book, *Single in the CIA*, is a memoir about her experience working in the National Clandestine Service (aka Directorate of Operations) of the Central Intelligence Agency. Her series, *Mingling in the CIA*, takes readers on a disturbing yet comical journey into the daily lives of the officers in America's premier spy agency.

She currently resides in Southern California with her husband and two children.

More information is available at www.shellymateer.com.